GUARDIANS OF TIME

BOOK 1

THE DOG SNATCHER

by
Phyllis Wheeler

Illustrated by
Katie O'Malley

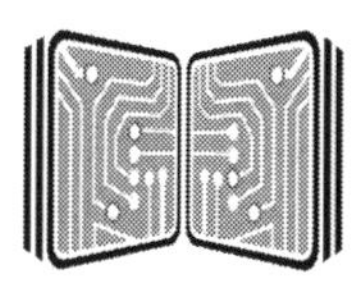

Motherboard Books

The Dog Snatcher: Guardians of Time Book 1 by Phyllis Wheeler
Illustrated by Katie O'Malley

Published by Motherboard Books
244 E. Glendale Rd.
St. Louis, MO 63119
www.MotherboardBooks.com

Cover illustrations by Katie O'Malley

Library of Congress Cataloging-in-Publication Data
An application to register this book for cataloging has been filed with the Library of Congress.
ISBN: 979-8-9866999-0-5

Here's what early readers are saying:

Eleven-year-old Caleb: "Great story! Time traveling in a clock shop was interesting, cool and funny!"

"A totally magical time-travel adventure, and a thrilling beginning to an exciting series!"—John Hendrix, New York Times bestselling illustrator and author

"I highly recommend this engaging chapter book. Your kids will enjoy it." —-Rob Currie, author of Hunger Winter: A WW2 Novel

"Time travel, alchemy, rich friendships, and a meaningful tale well told—what's not to like? —Wayne Thomas Batson, bestselling author of The Door Within Trilogy

Dedicated to my dear husband Steve, who makes my writing possible.

CHAPTER 1

I'M JAKE. I'M eleven. I love my parents, my dog, and my know-it-all twin sister. I'd do anything for them.

But sometimes I can't resist doing the wrong thing. That can lead to big trouble for everyone.

One summer evening, I stood at the end of our suburban driveway, staring. Something glittered on the pavement. It lay next to the big trash can I had just dragged out to the street.

Even in the shadow of the trash can I could tell it wasn't round like a coin.

What was it?

I picked up the strange object: a large silver and black key, its head covered with shiny seashell. It looked like the key to a pirate treasure chest. This is not the sort of thing you find in my neighborhood in St. Louis.

Maybe a rich person dropped it. No, there weren't any rich people in this neighborhood, full of small houses and big, old oak trees, now brushed by the warm winds of May.

But who else? I could see no one but Nicky, our little dog who shadowed my every move and even now nosed around the base of the trash can.

I stuck the key in my pocket and gave Nicky a pat. We walked back up the driveway. Nicky wagged his tail—he knew it was time for tennis balls in the backyard.

Do pirates throw tennis balls for their dogs?

I'd read and re-read Treasure Island. But maybe I'd been reading too much about pirates, I told myself as I stood on the backyard patio and threw the ball toward the fence, hard. Nicky raced after it, a blur of black, white, and brown, ears flying.

He brought the ball back, sat at my feet, and lifted his chin.

Nicky, a miniature Australian shepherd, was just the right size to pick up. But he hated being picked up. He was no lap dog and wanted to be in the thick of everything. He loved being alive.

He asked a question with his large bright eyes and dropped his tennis ball with a little thud onto the concrete.

My twin, Ava, poked her dark, curly head out the back door. People hardly ever guessed we were twins since I have blond hair. And even though we were both eleven, people told me I looked younger than her.

"Hey Jake, actually don't forget to take out the trash," she said.

"Already did," I said, and shrugged.

She closed the door and vanished, working on her chores no doubt.

I took a moment to pull out the key and admire it. It looked special. Very special. I'd never seen anything like it. It felt cold and smooth in my grip. My heartbeat sped up. It must be valuable. Would it make me rich?

This strange, ancient thing, maybe hundreds of years old—was it now mine? It seemed so. I turned it over in my hand twice.

I should show it to Dad, give it to Dad.

But I wanted it.

And I stuck it back in my pocket.

I just wanted to keep it.

CHAPTER 2

NICKY SNIFFED AT the night air for a long moment and then looked around.

From our back yard we could see over the fence to a sidewalk. A brown boxer walked with his person, so naturally Nicky started barking. The effort shook his small body. Silly, since he had known the dog since last summer.

Ava came out the back door, her white school blouse shining in the dusk like a pirate signal flag. "Hush, Nicky," she said. Then to me, "Time to go in."

I didn't keep much from her, but I didn't want to tell Ava about the key. At the moment, it was nobody's business but mine. Twins shared so much—toys, chores, friends—and maybe I wanted to keep something to myself.

Anyway, wherever it came from, she wasn't getting it.

The plan for the rest of the evening only aimed for more chores and then homework and practicing our band instruments. Ava and I were in no hurry—we cleaned up the supper dishes in our normal ultra-slow fashion.

We spread our notebooks across the dining room table. Dad, an Uber driver by day, prepared to answer math questions. He wandered over from his favorite chair in the living room, a newly sharpened pencil tucked behind his ear. I stared at my first math problem. I really wasn't ready—I hadn't listened in class. But he was.

It was a typical evening, nearing the end of the school term. Mom, as usual, was at work. Being a nurse in the ER was like that. She was gone a lot, nearly always until eleven in the evening.

The doorbell rang.

Nicky raced to the door, barking.

"Be quiet," I said at the same time as Ava. Nicky barked again.

Dad opened the door, running a hand through his brown hair and adjusting his sweatshirt. "Yes?" It was hard to hear his words with the barking. He frowned, looking out.

And then his pencil dropped.

Ava and I both crept closer to listen. Dad somehow managed to both pick up the pencil and shush Nicky, who crouched by his knee and whined.

In the evening light stood a skinny guy who looked a few years older than us, maybe fourteen years old, all arms and legs. His straight spiky black hair stuck out in all directions. He wore a black tee shirt and black jeans clasped by a big silver belt buckle.

The guy thrust his chin out and up. "Ach, I lost something just now," he said in a vaguely foreign accent. "A key. Did youse-all find my key? A special key. There is no other like it."

"I haven't found a key," said Dad.

But I had. I drew in my breath.

Dad went on, "Where do you think you lost it?"

"Vat about them." The stranger indicated us twins with a tilt of his head. It was a statement, not a question.

Dad turned to us, eyebrows raised. "Did you find his key?"

My hands felt clammy. It was mine, right? Finders keepers? "I, uh, haven't found any key that's not mine," I said.

Ava moved to stand beside me. "Me neither," she said.

"Nuh." The guy's tone showed he didn't believe us. "It is here. I am not a fool." He paused, and nobody answered.

His jaw clenched, and his nostrils flared. He spat out the words: "I know you have it. But, I vill be on my way." He stooped, grabbed Nicky, turned, and headed down the street at a run. Nicky wiggled like crazy, of course.

He'd stolen our dog. I was too startled to react at first. We all were.

I couldn't think fast enough. "Wait!" I called.

"You can't do that!" yelled Dad as he started out the door after him.

It was like in a movie. Only this was real.

CHAPTER 3

AVA AND I took off after Dad. But the dog snatcher was faster than any of us.

He ran along a row of tall bushes. Suddenly I couldn't see him, and apparently neither could Dad or Ava. We got closer and looked behind the hedge. Had the black of his shirt blended in with the bushes? No.

He was gone.

The three of us stared at each other.

"No!" wailed Ava. "I want Nicky!"

"That jerk just stole our dog!" exclaimed Dad. "We gotta call the cops." He pulled out his phone and punched in the numbers. He talked for a minute, gave our address, then hung up and headed for home.

Following him, I didn't say anything. But my dinner churned, and a big hollow place opened up inside somewhere. Nicky had been part of our family since we were in kindergarten. And now…

Dad closed the front door behind us with a thud.

Ava stared at Nicky's dog bed.

I stooped to pick up his rubber ducky and gave it a squeaky squeeze, then another. I knelt and put it on the carpet where Nicky would always pick it up. But it didn't move.

Nicky was gone.

I sank into a chair and closed my eyes. Why didn't I give up the key? Of course I wanted my dog more than some old dumb key.

In fact, it was all my fault that our dog was missing.

Why had I thought to call the key mine? Clearly it wasn't.

When you hurt someone, apologize and then try to make it right. Dad always said that. But how?

I'd lied to Dad. I'd hurt our family, big time. I needed to say something. I opened my mouth, but nothing came out.

I had no apology to give. Not even the simple word, "Sorry." I had nothing. Nada.

But I could search for Nicky. Yes.

How?

Ten agonizing minutes later, headlights flashed through the windows when a police officer showed up.

"Now, let's go over this again," said the officer, standing in the porchlight at the open front door with his notepad and pen.

He raised one eyebrow and checked his watch as we told him about the vanishing act.

Then he shook his head. "Folks, I don't know what to do with that. Let's give me something to work with. Footprints?"

He pulled out his flashlight and stepped off the porch.

"Maybe he stood here for a second," I said.

We examined the ground. But, because of the new garden mulch, we didn't find any footprints.

"Then he went that way down the street," I said.

The policeman checked his watch again and left, still shaking his head. He probably had other, more important work to do.

Dad flopped into his armchair, a scowl on his face.

Ava beckoned, then pulled me down the hallway to my room and closed the door behind us. Lemurs and sea otters stared at us with round eyes from my posters, and my fish tank hummed.

"You're not telling me something." She stood with hands on hips.

"Why do you think that?"

"You have a funny look on your face."

The lie inside gurgled in my stomach. But I wasn't ready to let go of it. "I told you already," I said. Oh, no, I was getting in deeper and deeper. I lowered my head.

"Are you sure?" she demanded.

"I just feel really bad about Nicky."

"We all do," she said. She cocked her head to the side and narrowed her eyes. "You know something."

I sighed. Twins are like that. I was busted. "I didn't think a guy would come to the house ..." I murmured.

She shook her head and tapped her foot.

"It's true," I said. "There really was a key."

She lifted an eyebrow. "I know."

"I found it in the street when I put the trash can out." I pulled it from my pocket. "I was thinking finders keepers."

The key lay there in my palm, cold, silvery black with pearly accents, full of secrets. Three inches long, bigger than any key had a right to be.

"You lost our Nicky for that old thing?" Her voice rose.

"I didn't know—"

"You keep messing things up." Ava poked her finger at my chest. "You got us kicked out of our old house. Now this."

"Tell me about it." Inner gremlins clutched my guts, tighter and tighter.

"You've got to return the key," she said.

"Take it." I tossed the key to her.

"I don't want it," she said.

"Keep it."

“You keep it.”

She ran a finger over the ornate surface. The yellow plastic beaded Hello Mellow bracelet that dangled from her wrist clattered against the metal. She looked closer. “This end of the key is covered with seashell,” she said. “I think they call this mother-of-pearl.”

“If it’s real,” I said, “it’s too big for any lock.” I sank down on my bed, head down. I was definitely having a bad day.

After a minute, she dropped the key back into my hand. I took a deep breath and stood up. At least I had the key. What could I do with it?

“It’s got to be good for something.” I waved it in the air. “ Maybe there’s a big old pirate chest somewhere that’s just the right size for this. Whaddayathink? Or the key to a castle. A big one, with giants.” I’d always loved fairy tales. So full of wild possibilities. I’d even put a castle into the fish tank in my room.

She shook her head, but my crazy thoughts made her crack a smile.

"Maybe it's to a dragon's treasure," I went on.

"You really need to get more serious, Jake."

"Oh, come on, you'd love it if we found a treasure chest."

"I'd love it if that key could help us find Nicky," she said.

"What if," I said, "there is a big lock right here in front of me. Like a locker. Only I can't see it." I thrust the key forward in the air and turned it to the left.

I must have done something. She was gone. Somehow I found myself in a small dark shop crammed with ticking clocks, so many that it was hard to move. It was another place.

CHAPTER 4

I STUMBLED FORWARD. A huge sinking feeling grabbed my belly as I caught myself on a table covered with small clocks. What had happened? Where was I? Where was Ava?

A balding man who faced me wearing a black cloak held out his hands in a "stop" gesture, palms out. He shook his head and uttered a stream of words. I heard the word "nine" spoken with emphasis. Wait. Did that mean "no" in some other language? His costume was just odd, like something you might see in a play. It felt unreal.

"Um, wait," said a brown-haired boy a bit older than me who faced me next to the man. He wore a St. Louis Cardinals tee shirt and jeans. "He looks like an American."

Maybe he had read my own St. Louis tee shirt, from the zoo.

The boy addressed me. "Do you—um—speak English?"

"That's where we are, America, right?" My voice trembled. Somehow I wasn't sure, though. I felt dizzy and disoriented—we could have been in a dusty clock shop anywhere on the planet.

"I am sorry," said the man, whose accent I couldn't place. "I vas saying, please do not move quickly around the shop or you vill break something."

"Ah, okay." I froze. It was the least I could do.

He looked relieved. "Allow me to introduce myself. I am an alchemist known as Paracelsus." He pronounced it PAIR-uh-SELL-sis. The man bowed slightly from the waist. "And no, you are not in America at the moment."

"I'm William," said the brown-haired boy. "Will Bosch. I grew up in, um, St. Louis. And you are ...?"

"I'm Jacob Reinhold. Jake. I'm from St. Louis, too." As if he couldn't tell from my tee shirt. But I didn't want to be obnoxious. The ticking and whirring of clocks surrounded me. Big booms and little chittering, and everything in between.

"How'd you get here?" asked Will.

I shrugged. "I have no idea, to be honest."

"A key!" Paracelsus pointed to my hand. "That is how you came here."

The key was still in the palm of my hand.

"That means you've come to the right place," the man went on. "You vouldn't have that key if ve veren't intended to help you." He pointed through the shop window at the sign out front. "Uhren Hueter. That means Guardians of Time."

This weirdness was a lot to digest, for someone who had just recently been tossing balls to his dog in his peaceful back yard. Shivers ran up and down my neck.

I suddenly felt very alone. I cleared my throat. "I wish the key had brought my sister, too. My twin sister, Ava. We were looking for our dog who got kidnapped. Er, dognapped. By someone who ran off down the street and then vanished. The police don't know what to do."

Paracelsus reached into a drawer and thrust another large key into my hand, this one fairly plain. "Here. Go back and bring Ava. She can use this key. Just hold up your key and turn it to the left, like unlocking the cabinet of a big grandfather clock. She vill do the same with hers."

* * *

Ava's mouth dropped open when she arrived, looking first at me and then at the other two. "Where are we?"

"Vell, ve are in our clock shop," Paracelsus said.

"I can see that." She wrinkled her nose.

"Out our front window you vill see a street in Vienna," said Paracelsus. "Sometimes the view is different. The day I met Will I could see St. Louis, Missouri, USA, North Broadway."

She snorted. "I don't believe we are in Vienna."

Paracelsus shrugged. "I suggest you step outside the shop."

Ava made her way to the front door, followed by Will and me. When she opened the door, I glimpsed the shop's sign, hung above us in the shape of a clock face. Chipped paint made it look bedraggled. The shop looked out on an alley. Damp, smelly air blew in. People passed by dressed in plain brown or black skirts or pants, and off-white shirts or blouses with dark brown vests and boots.

Hobbit costumes.

"For-sicht!" called a voice above us.

"Look out!" Will said. Just in time, he pulled Ava out of the way before a cascade of dirty water fell from above.

Round-eyed, Ava and I retreated to the store, followed by Will who closed the door behind us.

"That is not Vienna," said Ava, pointing to the window with a shaky finger. "Vienna is a much nicer city."

"It's Vienna in 1532," said Will.

CHAPTER 5
VIENNA, 1532

"I NEVER THOUGHT I'd be in Vienna. Or in 1532," said Ava. "I need to sit down."

My head spun. "Me too."

Paracelsus led us carefully through the shop to the office, where five wooden chairs shared the space with an old and cluttered desk. A flickering flame in a desk lamp cast wobbly light. A small round table piled with papers held an ash tray and a tobacco pipe, which gave off wisps of musty, sweet smoke.

As I sat, I closed my eyes. "I thought the world is a simple place," I said. "What you see is what you get. People don't vanish. I don't find myself in strange new places all of a sudden." I opened my eyes. The four of us sat in a semicircle, looking like a reasonably normal bunch of people—except for Paracelsus' black cloak with a white lace ruffle at the throat. No, we weren't a reasonably normal bunch of people. Not with Paracelsus sitting there, bald head shining in the lamplight.

"Many things," said Paracelsus, "are not what they seem. Many people, too."

Ava and I lifted eyebrows at each other.

"So, currently we are in Vienna, 1532," said Ava.

"Correction. Outside that door, it is Vienna, 1532," said Paracelsus. An amused smile hung around his lips. He scratched his head and leaned forward. "But in here, it is different. The clock shop travels through time and space, and its door can open out in any number of places.

"You see, it is the headquarters for our guild, the Guardians of Time. The guild members can get to it from a variety of places in space and time, without the need for a key."

"What's a guild?" I asked.

"An association of merchants or craftsmen who work together," said Paracelsus. "For the Guardians of Time Guild, ve help people who are lost in time. Original members, such as I, are alchemists from Europe in the years 1300 to 1600 or so. Ve also have apprentices such as Will."

"Are you that old?" asked Ava skeptically.

"With our work assignment comes certain power and ability. One of those is being granted a long, long life," said Paracelsus.

"So ..." I was so confused, I didn't even know what to ask.

Ava dove in. "How many people get lost in time? A lot?"

"Five or six every year, at least," said Paracelsus. "Just last week we rescued a man from Finland, 2022, who went fishing and encountered a fold in space-time. He found himself treading water in ancient Greece, watching a sea battle between Greeks and Persians. Flaming timbers fell all around him. He vas glad to make it home in one piece … with our help."

This idea of being lost worried me. "Who gets lost?" I asked.

"My father got lost," said Will, "and Paracelsus found him."

"You think that's what happened with our dog?" I asked.

"Tell us what happened," said Will.

We told the story—the true story—interrupting each other as usual.

"I should have given him the key," I mumbled. "It wasn't mine. I always mess everything up." I huddled down into my chair, shoulders slumped.

"How could you know he would steal your dog?" asked Paracelsus.

"Hmm." I didn't feel any better.

"Describe the kidnapper," said Paracelsus.

"Fourteen years old, maybe," said Ava. "Long arms and legs. Straight black hair sticking out in all directions. Black tee shirt and jeans and a cool silver belt buckle. Talks with an accent, possibly German."

"Wow," said Will. "You sound like, um, a detective or something."

"Precisely. Sherlock Holmes is my hero," she said.

Paracelsus pulled a book off a bookshelf in the office and opened it. "Does this look like him?" We crowded around him and stared at a drawing of a man with straight black hair sticking out

M.ORTOLAN

everywhere and black eyes full of challenge. But it was a man, not a boy.

"Yes!" Ava said. "That is his dad, maybe."

"Yup, I think so too," I said.

"That is the alchemist Martin Ortolan," said Paracelsus. "He broke his Guild vows to protect and save, and began luring people to get lost in time. For fun as far as I can tell. For punishment he has to live for eons as a teenager. He has been a problem for us for centuries."

"Um, I guess he's stealing dogs," said Will.

"And losing keys," I said.

"So, where is he? And actually what did he do with Nicky?" demanded Ava.

"What do we do next?" I asked.

CHAPTER 6

VIENNA, 1532

PARACELSUS, HIS BACK to the bookcase, locked his hands behind him and balanced on his toes.

"Martin Ortolan," he said, "has certain places he likes to hide. Usually caves. The first place he may go is to his supposed hideout in Lyon, France, 1680. That is the easiest one for him to get to since he has lost his key. I suggest that Will take you to look for it."

"Wait," said Ava. "If Martin has other ways to time-travel, why is he so interested in this key?"

Paracelsus held up three fingers. "There are three vays to time-travel that I have discovered," he declared. "First, using a key. Second, stepping into the clock shop and operating its controls." He nodded toward a bank of long metal levers and leather straps visible to one side in the clock room through the office doorway.

"Third, using special hand gestures. That one is reserved only for the alchemists, full Guild members, not apprentices. Martin Ortolan has lost his privilege to do this."

He wagged a fourth finger, his pinkie. "And, there is a way to travel not in time and space, but simply in space. Martin Ortolan invented that as a Guild member, and now that he is disgraced somehow still is allowed to use it. He translocates—that is, he vanishes from one place and reappears in another, all in the same time period. Ve think it has something to do with his key."

"Did you want to see his key?" I pulled it out of my pocket and held it out.

Paracelsus picked it up, examined it, and returned it to me. He pointed to a tiny grimacing face stamped into it, near the top of the shaft. "Yes, his key carries the special Ortolan mark. It must govern this ability to translocate. This must be how he escaped from you, as he was running away holding the dog."

"But he didn't have the key, I did," I said.

Ava shook her head and smiled. "Apparently it works even if the key is at a distance," she said. "Wait, is this Martin's key now or your key?" She was addressing Paracelsus.

"When he was a Guild member in good standing, it vas his key. When he vent astray, I took it away. Then he stole it back. That was around four hundred years ago," he said.

"So…" I said. "Do you want it back now?" I held it out again.

Paracelsus sighed. "I vish we could solve the problem of Martin Ortolan by taking away his key. No, I do not vant it anymore." He lightly pushed my hand away. "Use it vell. Get your dog back."

He glanced at his pocket watch and cleared his throat. "And now, it's time for me to monitor the queenship succession in ancient Cush." He pronounced it as if was part of the word cushion.

"Cush?" I asked.

"Pardon, that is an old name for the region upriver from Egypt, known in your time as Sudan. I have received a letter. Things are uncertain: who vill be the next Queen of Sheba in the year 945 BC? So I am afraid that I vill have to excuse myself. William can take care of you vell." He shook hands all around, bowed slightly from the waist, and stood straight. He quickly fanned his fingers, and then he vanished.

Will shook his head. "It's like those hand signals baseball catchers use."

I imitated the hand gesture, but nothing happened when I did it.

"So, how do we find our dog?" asked Ava.

"I'm learning more about the ways to travel to, um, specific points in place and time," said Will. He led us into the clock room and rested a hand on a foot-long metal lever that stuck out from the collection of levers that, along with gears and leather straps, formed the device in the corner. "To travel using this shop, you use the levers to direct it to go to certain places. The shop moves through space and time. Sort of like a TARDIS, you know, the police call box on Doctor Who."

Ava and I both nodded.

"But," he went on, "it's hard to pinpoint exactly when and where you're going to end up, unless it's one of the shop's regular stops, like here in 1532 Vienna."

"Stops?" asked Ava.

"Yes, like bus stops," said Will. "Or if you trust the Guiding Hand to take you where you need to go, um, you turn your key in the air. That's how Paracelsus found my dad. That's how you got here."

"The Guiding Hand?" I asked. A willy ran up my spine.

Will grinned. "That's what Paracelsus calls him. The one that's in charge of Time, who directs the Guardians of Time."

Did I know about this being from church? I had a feeling I did.

"Where did Paracelsus find your dad?" asked Ava.

"He was a prisoner in a Native American village in about 1200 AD."

I whistled. "Wow."

"We have got to find Nicky," said Ava. "I don't want that person, that Martin, mistreating him."

A creak came from the other room, then a light "plop."

"The mail slot," said Will. He headed for the front room, Ava and I following. We carefully maneuvered through the shop to the front door. Will stepped over a letter lying on the floor, opened the door, and looked both ways. "Just checking. Nobody's there." He sounded oddly unsurprised.

The old-timey cursive writing said, "Jacob and Ava." At least, maybe it said that.

"Go ahead, open it," said Will.

I picked it up carefully and slid my finger under the edge of the envelope. It was sealed with red wax that held the imprint of a grimacing face. The Ortolan mark.

I broke the seal, unfolded the thick coarse paper, and read aloud from hand-drawn letters that sprawled across the page, as if written by pirates.

"Give my special key and get dog back. No key, no dog. 5 days until I finish the dog. Post the key to PO Box 100177, St. Louis, Missouri, 63101."

Could Martin "finish" Nicky? Yes, he could.

Oh, man. This couldn't be happening. He couldn't, wouldn't, do that to my dog.

A cuckoo clock behind me bleated like a lost lamb.

My hands trembled, holding the letter. My eyes stung. I rubbed them and took a deep breath. Ava gripped my shoulder.

Chapter 7
Vienna, 1532

NO!" AVA PULLED away and stamped her foot. Her furious eyes bored into mine. "We're getting Nicky back. Now."

I shook my head and clenched my eyes shut. Regret pooled in my belly again. Now, why had I lied?

"I don't need this key." I dangled it from my fingers. "My life was fine without it."

Images flooded my mind. Nicky with his alert eyes, running after a ball with joy so visible in the tilt of his black ears. Nicky cuddling up in my bed at night, snuggled against my knee on the Spiderman comforter, sharing space with my stuffed wallaby.

Nicky hanging out in Ava's purple room, twitching his ears at the classical music spilling from her headphones. Nicky trotting with self-importance on his leash as we took a turn around our block. Nicky allowing the chatty elderly neighbors to pet him.

Nicky was in danger. What could we do?

Will stood there on the rough rope doormat of the clock shop. "Um, what if you mail the key and Martin doesn't give back the dog? Maybe he's lying. Maybe Nicky is already … dead."

Ava closed her eyes and then opened them. "Nicky is not dead."

"Why do you say that?" I asked.

"I just know it," she said. "Maybe it's my sixth sense."

I rolled my eyes. Everybody knows there's no such thing as a sixth sense. We only have five senses. But I didn't feel like arguing with her. She was right a lot of the time.

"What if," Will asked, "Martin is stuck in St. Louis because he doesn't have the key?"

"But he just put a letter through the door slot. He has to be in Vienna," I said.

Will shook his head. "I bet he went to the shop doorway in Old North St. Louis and dropped the letter through the mail slot. It would automatically send the letter to the shop here." He held up both hands. "I know, I know, it's hard to understand. But I bet he was never anywhere near Vienna."

"How about you?" Ava asked Will. "Can you travel without a key or the clock shop?"

"I'm just an apprentice. So I have to use a key or the shop. Just like you." He pulled a five-inch key covered with spidery etchings out of his pocket, bigger and cooler than the one in my pocket.

"Awesome," we said at the same time.

"Um, my key is a gift from my grandfather. I thought he had died, but I've found that he is a Guardian of Time apprentice too." His voice carried a ring of pride. "Of course he can't be a Guardian of Time because he never was a medieval alchemist, so he's an apprentice as long as he wants to be. I haven't met my granddad yet in these time travels. But I will soon. I just know it. It's my dream to go to a Cardinals game with him."

Ava got that faraway look in her eyes. "Martin Ortolan broke his vows," she said. "So he should not be a Guild member any more. Should not be able to time travel any more. Should not have a key at all. Right?"

Will shrugged. "Um, seems like you're right. But we're not the ones who decide."

"So, what do we do now?" I asked.

We trooped back to the office. Ava cleared her throat. "Maybe we should go home. Certainly Mom is getting home from work and wondering where we are."

My stomach dropped. The lie. The time was coming up for me to confess it to Dad. And I didn't know if I could do it.

"When you time travel, you normally return just an instant after you left," said Will. "No matter how long you are gone. Um, usually that's how it works."

Ava took a deep breath, and I did too. Maybe we didn't have to go back right away after all.

"Where could Martin go next?" I asked.

"Um, he can't go much of anywhere without the key. Unless he comes here to the shop," said Will.

In the other room, the front door banged open. After a short pause, it banged again.

"What was that?" asked Ava.

After we dodged clocks again to get to the front door, we looked out. The view showed a different city. We saw an alleyway, narrower than the one in Vienna. Instead of tan stone buildings on a sunny day in Vienna, here they were painted a bright shade of pink. And here it rained.

"Oh, no. Martin has done it." Will shook his head. "He must have entered the shop through its doorway in St. Louis, adjusted the levers real quick, and gone out somewhere else. Like Paracelsus said, he's got a hideout in Lyon in the middle of France in 1680, so we're probably in Lyon." (He pronounced it lee-OHN.) "The shop, um, often opens out at that time and place. A favorite stop."

L'HORLOGE
ARRÊT DU TEMPS

The three of us stared out into the wet alleyway. Passersby in hobbit costumes similar to the ones in Vienna got wet in the rain, including a small child towed by his mother's hand. He looked at us with wide eyes as they passed by.

I'd been in old Vienna, now old France. None of it looked very comfortable.

"Um, maybe Martin keeps another key in his hideout here," said Will. "Maybe he's going to get it."

"Should we stop him?" asked Ava.

"If we can get there in time," said Will.

"What about Nicky? I didn't hear him in the shop just now," I said.

Ava clenched her eyes shut. "Nicky is alive. I know it. We have five days. Let's go."

CHAPTER 8
LYON, 1680

OUTSIDE THE CLOCK shop doorway, we slipped out into the rain. Pink and yellow four- and five-story buildings loomed above us as dim light reached into the canyon between them.

Before we left, Will had found some yellow plastic ponchos somewhere in the shop to cover our tee shirts and jeans. So we weren't getting wet, but in our bright yellow we looked wildly different from the drab crowds of people walking past.

They didn't stare. They just trudged by in the rain with glum faces. Probably we were the least of their worries.

"Pardon," said a man dressed all in black, with an odd haircut shaved on top, as he brushed past. Only it didn't sound like "pardon" in English. The emphasis was on the second syllable, par-DOH.

That questionable smell was back, too. Was it horse dung? I wrinkled my nose at Ava, and she wrinkled her nose back.

Two men walked past, muttering at each other. Not in English.

"Lyon?" asked Ava. "Is it Lyon?"

Will shrugged. "Um, I think so. They're speaking French. My dad taught me some, and I'm learning more. Dad knows several languages. These could be silk workers. That's who lived in Lyon in 1680, people making beautiful silk tapestries on special looms for the palaces of the kings and queens of Europe. That's what Paracelsus told me last time we were here."

"Like what kings and queens?" I asked. "Real ones?"

"Real ones, like the series of French kings named Louis (LOO-EE) at Versailles (ver-SIGH). The most famous one was called the Sun King."

Ava nodded. "That was Louis the Fourteenth. I actually know about him because of all the classical music he sponsored. It's on my baroque playlist."

"Um, right now, in 1680, he is the one on the throne," said Will.

"Wow," said Ava, bobbing her head. "I wish I could see him. Meet him."

We dodged puddles and pedestrians.

"Hey, you ever go to baseball games?" asked Will over his shoulder.

"We go once a year when the summer library program gives us free tickets," I said.

“I love baseball,” Will said. “But Dad’s moved to a native American village about 800 years in the past, and we never get to go anymore. But I do get to go to a different kind of ball game with Dad. Chunkey. So I guess it’s okay.”

His lopsided grin was less than 100 percent enthusiastic. Clearly his Cardinals tee shirt spoke volumes. He was a fan, through and through. And he couldn’t get to the games!

We paused in front of a dark building. Brown paper or something like it formed its front window. I looked closer. Maybe it was oiled cloth, like the crafts teacher used at summer camp.

The sign outside consisted of a portrait of a pony on a round plate hanging over the side-walk. But since there were no cars, no horses, only pedestrians, the narrow street was really all sidewalk.

“This is an inn,” said Will. “I think.”

A woman in a long brown skirt and blouse came out of the inn. She carried a broom and lifted an eyebrow at us as she began sweeping the street.

"Par-DOHN," said Will.

She stopped sweeping.

"Ou? Where?" he asked. He gestured all around.

They carried on a brief conversation, Will waving his arms a lot.

Will turned to us. "We're in France, all right." he said. "We are in Lyon."

He turned back to her. "Chien? Dog?" He pronounced it shee-EHN.

She shook her head. "Beaucoup de chiens," she said.

"Lots of dogs," Will translated. As if in response, a slender, long-legged dog of medium size eased around the corner and nosed a bit of garbage on the other side of the little street.

"Chien," she said, and pointed, wrinkling her nose. She didn't think much of the dog. Garbage-eaters couldn't be popular.

"Let's look around. Clearly we won't find Nicky by standing still," Ava said.

Downhill led to the bank of a river. We waved at the woman who talked to us before we set out the other way, up the street, climbing the hill.

"This is one of two hills in Lyon," said Will. "They are full of caves. Two rivers meet here. It's an old city, settled by the Romans."

Hmm, a great place for a time-traveler to explore. But, never mind. How were we going to find our dog?

CHAPTER 9
LYON, 1680

I WALKED WITH Will and Ava up the hill as the rain let up. We headed for Martin's hideout, or where Will thought Martin's hideout was. We climbed crooked, tiny streets and carefully avoided stepping in the mucky gutter in the middle. Big stone "bricks" formed the paving material.

In 1680 Lyon right then, plenty of people were going somewhere, on foot, dressed in brown, black, and off-white.

We took off our yellow ponchos and stashed them under our elbows. The weather remained cool. With the end of the rain, a succession of smells collided in my nose. Mildew. Flowers in window boxes. There was the musky smell of a sweating horse pulling a cart full of black chunks—coal? And, all around, human body odor, like in gym class.

"I am not sure I can stand to be here," said Ava. "It smells so bad."

"We can't abandon Nicky because it stinks here!" I rolled my eyes.

She shook her head and continued to follow Will. "Hey, when were you here before, Will?"

"Um, Paracelsus took me here not long ago. We were chasing Martin that time too, looking for a missing book. It was easier with Paracelsus helping, since he can use his sixth sense to follow the tracker on Martin's key. I can't seem to do that yet. But we didn't catch Martin. He was always one step ahead of us. Anyway, I've been an apprentice for a couple of years, and have been lots of places now."

"Do you go to school, too?" asked Ava.

"Dad homeschools me. We have a stack of books, and every now and then I go back to the 2020s in St. Louis to get more. My best friend collects them for me."

Two blocks away, up the hill, I noticed a black-haired skinny guy in a loose brown robe, dressed like Friar Tuck. He bent over to address a dog, holding its collar. It was a brown, black, and white dog of small size, ears pricked forward.

"Nicky!" The word burst out of Ava's and my mouths at the same time.

It was Martin wearing the robe. So that was his current disguise.

Nicky dove in our direction, ears up, eyes bright. He looked like he was going for the gold. Yes! We'd found him! And he had found us!

But Martin's hand on his collar restrained him. Martin grabbed him, gathered the hem of his robe in one hand, and took off running. Nicky struggled to no avail.

I'd been here before, and I would not to let it happen again. My feet seemed to grow wings as I charged up the street, and I heard Ava and Will's footfalls behind me. It was a race I was determined to win.

Martin, though taller, couldn't run as fast as I could in that robe, I just knew it. He also had to get people to move aside, while the ranks of onlookers were already parted for me. We raced through narrow street after narrow street, always uphill. We passed a small square, and another.

My heart thumped in my ears. Panting, we chasers had to slow our pace a bit. But then, Martin did too.

The sky opened up; there were no more tall buildings. We charged up to a bowl-shaped stone amphitheater on a grassy hillside. It wasn't as big as a baseball stadium, but it was big enough for thousands of people. Some of the stately stone columns decorating it had fallen down. They had to be old, very old. Roman, probably.

Martin darted into the ruins, and we dashed after him. He charged up the stepped pathway and then ran along one of the large curved benches. I stumbled once over a loose stone and had to slow down. But I didn't stumble more than that. The ancient theater was in surprisingly good shape, considering it must be 2,000 years old.

Nicky struggled as he bounced on Martin's shoulder, watching us. He wasn't happy. And I wasn't happy.

Was I close enough to offer the key for him?

"Hey!" I called. "Do you want your key?"

But all the running took my breath away, and my words came out in a whisper.

So Martin led us back from the Roman ruins to the city streets. I was looking right at him when he pivoted and darted into a large stone church. We charged in after him and stood panting in the enormous cool, dark interior.

It was quiet. Too quiet.

A robed man walked towards us, his footfalls echoing against the vast curved ceiling, sculpted into arches that reminded me of a parade of open umbrellas. Five or ten people sat or knelt in the pews in the center with their heads bowed.

What must he think of three strangely dressed kids, ponchos under our arms, panting and looking around?

We interrupted the prayerful quiet space, I realized. I ducked my head apologetically.

"Pardon. Nous cherchons," said Will. "We're looking for … un homme, a man. Avec un chien. With a dog."

The man shook his head, and a stream of words fell from his lips.

Will nodded and turned towards us. "He says no one else has recently come in."

I took a deep trembling breath. Ava's face crumpled with disappointment.

"We were so close," I whispered. My words echoed in the soaring room as emptiness settled into my insides. I'd lost Nicky. Lost him for me, and for Ava.

The man made the sign of the cross in the air at us and spoke a few more words. It seemed to be a blessing, and it brought me some peace. Following Will's lead, we bowed to him, thanked him, and left.

CHAPTER 10
LYON, 1680

STILL CATCHING OUR breaths, we filed out of the church—L'Eglise de Saint-Just, according to the sign. "Church of Saint Just," said Will. The afternoon had turned downright sunny, with a breeze chasing clouds across the sky.

"I don't get it," said Will, turning to face back the way we'd come. "Martin shouldn't be able to vanish like that without a key. Um, I know Paracelsus can do that with a wave of his fingers. But not Martin, after he was demoted."

I scratched my head. "Didn't somebody say something about the Ortolan mark on Martin's key? That using that even from a distance he can translocate?"

"Precisely," said Ava. She bobbed her head.

"Oh, yeah," said Will.

The three of us walked slowly down the massive stone steps, worn by countless feet.

My stomach rumbled. All this running around was making me hungry.

"What can we do about food?" asked Ava.

"Um, I don't have any money," said Will. "We keep snacks at the clock shop. We'll get back there eventually."

"Are we giving up on Nicky?" I asked. My hands clenched.

"No, no, not at all," said Will. "I have an idea of where Martin will go next. Remember we were looking for his hideout? We'll keep looking now."

"Right." I relaxed. Some.

Will led us through the city streets across the top of the massive hill, moving more slowly this time, but still in a hurry. Soon we reached the lower hillside, the familiar part of town, crowded with the usual four- and five-story buildings of yellow and pink. Pigeons fluttered on the rooftops, cooing a greeting. I relaxed, sort of.

"The hideout is in the catacombs under this part of Lyon," said Will. "I've looked for it before, with Paracelsus. I have a good idea of where it is."

He turned left onto a narrower street. "We're looking for a big door. It's right along here somewhere." He examined the doorways in a large building on one side.

"This?" I pointed to a heavy door, rounded on top, with a wrought-iron handle right in the middle.

"Yes, that's it. A traboule is a special passageway through buildings and courtyards. This part of Lyon is full of them. Many are hidden." He pulled open the heavy door, and sure enough, behind it was an indoor version of the street behind us, with a floor made of stone bricks and covered by an arched ceiling.

In half-darkness the passageway stretched forward toward a sunlit courtyard not far away. Our footfalls slapped against the stones, and water trickled faintly in the distance.

When the heavy door behind us slammed, it shut out the street noise. It felt too quiet. I shivered.

The huge door slammed again behind us and broke the spell. A large man in a leather apron charged past, shoving us out of the way. "Pardon, pardon," he rumbled impatiently. Soon he'd gone beyond where we could see.

"We need to pick up the pace," said Will. "So we can catch up to Martin." We walked faster.

The dim passageway widened into a tiny courtyard open to the sky four stories up. At one end stood a stone fountain where water dribbled out of the mouth of a skinny fish into a small pool. The other end of the courtyard held a set of spiral stone stairs leading down into darkness.

Chapter 11
Lyon, 1680

I LED THE three of us as we clattered down the spiral stairwell. My shoe slipped, and I caught myself on the rough wall.

"Hey, slow down," said Ava.

The stone steps twisted always to the right. Pretty soon the light faded. I brushed a sweaty hand through my hair. I'd never been too happy about the dark.

“This isn’t the basement,” said Ava. “It’s deeper.”

“Anybody got a cell phone?” asked Will. “We can use them one at a time as flashlights. Hopefully that will last us long enough.”

I pulled out my phone. No bars, of course. Why was I even checking? I turned on its flashlight and continued to lead the way down.

“Um, we’re heading for the catacombs,” said Will. His voice echoed.

I had to ask. “What’s a catacomb?”

“Underground space, dug by human hands,” said Will. “Sort of like a network of tunnels. The Romans and others made them. Personally I think it’s easy to get lost in them.”

The word “lost” hung in the air for too long. I shivered.

“Caves, like in St. Louis,” said Ava. “They say our city is built on caves. Actually, that is where the breweries kept their beer cold, before refrigeration.

But there is no way to visit those caves now. You just hear rumors about them."

"Maybe that's why Martin was in St. Louis," I said. "He figured out how to get in."

The steps ended, and ahead of us stretched a level passageway. Cool air, not cold, flowed over me. My eyes had adjusted to the dimness, lit by the phone. The floor felt rough beneath my sneakers, as if the steps and passageway had been cut from the rock.

"These are the catacombs of Lyon," said Will. "Paracelsus said that originally they were probably for burial. Then people hid in them from time to time. Or maybe stored treasure in them."

We shuffled on. The darkness and silence pressed in like a pillow to the face. I felt like a trespasser.

Five minutes passed.

We reached a side passage. Should we take it?

Will paused. "I think we turned here," he finally said. He stepped into the lead. "I wish my sixth sense was stronger. He's surely got a spare key at his hideout, and it has a tracker on it of course. So I'm trying to locate it. Paracelsus was homing in on that when we were here before."

We turned down the narrower side tunnel. Will had to stoop, I could see in the bobbing light of my cell phone flashlight. We walked for ten minutes at least, as quietly as we could.

A soft male voice echoed along the tunnel. "Ach, du liebe. I must get back my special key. The one that takes me where I vant to go. Not this old thing." Something clinked. A key tossed to the stone floor?

I heard a whine and then a bark. It was my dog! He heard us!

I raced forward. "Nicky!" I called. "Nicky!"

Another bark, not close but not far.

I led the charge toward Nicky. The light from my phone wobbled like crazy as we raced forward.

The clatter from our feet sounded like ten people, not three.

"Nicky! Nicky!" we called.

Nothing.

We stumbled on. Which way?

"Nicky!" I called again.

No answer.

"Um, Martin probably picked up that spare key," mumbled Will. "Took off for some other place, some other time."

No sound but his voice echoed in the tunnel.

He was gone. My dog was gone. My numb fingers dropped my cell phone, and the flashlight winked out. We stood in darkness, heavy and thick.

Guilt pressed in on me like the darkness. I'd done it, nobody but me. A more honest person wouldn't even be in this dark place. And I couldn't undo it. My lie hung over my head like an executioner's axe.

I leaned back against the rough rock wall, my arms and legs trembling. I slid to the floor, pulled down by a huge sense of loss. “No,” I whispered. “No.”

Ava turned on the flashlight in her phone and knelt beside me. She grabbed my hand. Her firm grip felt comforting.

The sun shone high in the sky by the time we stumbled out again into the crowded streets of Lyon. More light reached the street, and some people looked almost cheerful now that the rain had ended. Two skinny dogs hovered in a dark corner as we passed, sniffing at something.

What would we do now? We couldn’t give up. Could we? I felt listless, like a ship with no wind in its sails.

Was that scumbag Martin feeding Nicky? Brushing him?

The crowd swelled and drew us along. Somebody a block away tootled on a flute. Kids chattered, and the previously unsmiling people broke out in grins. They were all going somewhere. What was happening?

A little puppet stage appeared, set up right there on the side of the little street.

"Let's watch," I called out. "Just for a minute."

The hand-sized puppets carried sticks and did their best to hit each other. "Biff!" said one. "Non!" cried the other. They pummeled each other with words, too, a stream of language I didn't understand. The crowd tittered at points, guffawed at others. It looked like one puppet was getting the worst of it. Wait, no, he was coming around to hit the other guy from behind. I laughed, along with all the others.

"It's just Punch and Judy," said Will, tugging at us. "C'mon, let's go,"

Footsteps pounded the pavement, loud even against the noise of the crowd and the puppeteers. Someone ran into me from behind, knocking us both down. "Pardon, pardon!" called a scruffy blond teenager as he untangled himself—and then took off.

"Uh oh," said Will. "Paracelsus warned me about this. That was probably a pickpocket."

I searched my pockets hurriedly.

Indeed, my cell phone was gone.

And the precious key.

Nicky had four days to live. And I had no way to ransom him.

CHAPTER 12
LYON, 1680

BACK AT THE clock shop, only the ticking and whirring of clocks kept the three of us company. The faint smell of pipe tobacco tinged the air in the office—and along with it the odor of failure.

"A pickpocket," I moaned as I stuffed my rumpled poncho underneath a chair. "Now I don't even have the key. I'll never see Nicky again. How could I have done this?"

My words got no answer. Will pulled some granola bars out of a desk drawer and handed them around. Then he pulled three medium-sized clocks from a box in the corner, along with some tools. "They don't work," he said. "While we figure out what's next, let's see if we can fix them."

Ava sat down with one in her lap, her forehead creased in concentration. Will put another one on the desk and gestured to me. "Take a look." He picked up one for himself and sat in a chair.

Paracelsus entered the office. Had he just now appeared in the other room, and I hadn't seen him? Apparently.

"Things in Cush have stabilized for the moment, and so I thought I vould come back and see how you are doing." He sat down in one of the chairs.

We wasted no time in filling him in, while tinkering with the clocks.

"A pickpocket took the key? That is a setback." He adjusted the lace at his throat. "Now tell me why, young Jacob, you think this is your fault," he said. His bald head shone in the lamplight.

"Everything bad is always my fault," I said. "I do dumb things." I poked at the sick clock, which responded by shooting a spring at me. "I never do anything right. It's always been that way. It got a lot worse a while back when I managed to get us evicted from our house."

"Oh?" asked Paracelsus.

"I was washing the dishes after supper." I picked up the screwdriver. "The doorbell rang, and I answered it. It was my buddy Roger. So I went out on the porch, then on outside. I forgot to turn off the water—the water in the kitchen sink." I offered a tired shrug. "You can guess what happened." My voice faltered.

Paracelsus reached over and patted my arm. "Go on."

"The water ran for like an hour and made a huge mess. They had to replace the kitchen floor." I stared at my feet. "Then the landlord kicked us out, and we had to go find another place. I've said I'm sorry, but I've never been able to make it right, never been able to make it up to the family. Nobody has ever let me forget it. It's just too big ..."

Ava pulled the back off her clock and looked up. "The bad part is, the new house we're renting has only one bathroom, not two."

"Yeah, so they all grumble about me when they have to stand in line," I said. "It stinks."

Ava glanced at me. "Sorry."

She poked a finger at the exposed gears in the back of the clock. "I wonder if we can change what happened about that," she said. "Since we're time-traveling anyway."

"What?" I took a deep breath, then another one. Could what I did be changed?

"Um, sure," said Will. "We could find that point in time where Jake didn't turn the water off. And we could sneak in and turn it off." He adjusted something on the back of his clock.

"Really?" My voice squeaked. I turned away from the clock on the desk to face the room.

No. It was a silly idea for lots of reasons. Changing history, for example.

Ava tugged at something inside her clock and echoed my thought. "I suppose the question is, how much can we tinker with history?"

Paracelsus touched his fingertips together. "Vell, it is a good question, how far ve can go. Changing major events? No. Ve are not allowed, and in fact I think ve cannot do it. But clearly ve are permitted to do small things. The Guild could not work otherwise. Will's father, for example. He lives in a Native American village in 1200 A.D. That seems to be allowed. Surprising but true."

The water incident wasn't a small thing to me! "Okay, so I go back to my house on the right day and sneak in there? What if I run into my younger self?" I asked.

Paracelsus shook his head. "In all my years of rescuing people lost in time, I have never seen that happen. If it did …" His voice trailed off, then resumed. "If you run into yourself, you should have a memory of doing that already. Do you?"

"No," I said.

"Under Guild rules, we have to abide by that. So you must stay out of sight or otherwise fool your younger self. If you break Guild rules, as Martin Ortolan did, you vill face penalties. In your case, perhaps erasing part of your memory. An accidental time traveler such as you has made no Guild vows and can't be held to a higher standard. But there are limits."

I didn't want part of my memory erased. I didn't want anybody tinkering with my brain, no sirree.

Ava shook her head too.

"What if we go back and get the water turned off?" I asked. "Then—no moving to another house?"

Paracelsus wagged his head from side to side. "Maybe yes, maybe no. It might happen anyway, for a different reason."

"But I wouldn't be the one to blame," I said.

"Likely," he said.

I sighed and poked at the clock on the desk. "I don't know what to do with this clock," I said. It was too complicated. Like my life.

CHAPTER 13
LYON, 1680

PARACELSUS STOOD UP. "We must retrieve the lost key as soon as possible. With its tracker tuned to the sixth sense, I should be able to find it. Will, it seems, still needs more practice."

Will frowned. "Yeah, I figured you were testing me, sending us chasing Martin and his spare key with only me in charge." He put his clock on the desk.

Paracelsus clapped him on the shoulder. "Peace, Will. You did vell."

Ava bounced to her feet. "So, what does a tracker look like?" She put her clock on the desk beside mine and Will's. Hers looked tidy and put together. It seemed all fixed. So did Will's. Mine, not so much.

Will pulled open a small drawer in the desk. "Like these trackers here."

We peered inside. Twenty or thirty flat black chips piled in a corner of the drawer. It looked like a pile of guitar picks for mice.

"Take one," said Paracelsus. "You can use it for practice."

I stuck one in my pocket, and Ava did likewise. You never know when you might need a mouse guitar pick.

"Apply one to a key or some other object, and it joins with the object. It becomes part of it," said Paracelsus.

I nodded, eyes wide. "And … ?"

"It speaks to your sixth sense. Remember, we all have a sixth sense," said Paracelsus. "A sixth sense tells you things you can't otherwise know from your regular five senses. It might warn you of danger. It might tell you your loved one far away is sick. It might tell you it's time to get up in the morning."

"Yes!" said Ava. "I have that. Like, I know Nicky is alive. I just know it."

"Yes, like that," said Paracelsus.

Ava pulled out her borrowed key and examined it. "I don't see a tracker on here."

"Um, you won't see it," said Will. "But it's there."

Impressive! "So, you can find where the pick-pocket is with that key, right now?" I asked.

Paracelsus nodded. "We vill just go for a walk. I vill search for it using my sixth sense. Perhaps our pickpocket has taken it to a pawn shop. But, maybe not. Ve should go before Martin realizes ve lost the key and starts using his sixth sense to search for it. Ve want to beat him there."

"Um, wait a sec," said Will. He pulled open another desk drawer. "I should show them the Babel chips too." In the drawer lay more guitar picks for mice. These were clear, not black.

"What are those?" asked Ava.

"Babel chips attach to your key and translate for you," said Paracelsus. "So you can understand if you put one on your key and hear someone speaking another language." He picked up two and handed them to Ava and me. "Here, put these on your keys."

We did so. The chips vanished as they joined with the keys.

"But not for Will?" I asked.

"Will is doing fine without one," said Paracelsus. "He's learning French. That's the better vay."

Will grinned. "Let's go."

We headed out again, four of us this time, Paracelsus in the lead. He moved surprisingly fast for someone with a pot belly, and we scrambled to keep up. He came to an intersection, lifted his head to look here and there, and then headed off.

The people in the streets took absolutely no notice of him. Apparently his cloak was a pretty normal thing to wear. In fact, we saw some others dressed similarly.

As for us, as before, people just didn't really seem to focus on us. We slipped through the city in his wake. Maybe we looked so unusual that they couldn't take us in.

"Here," he announced in front of a shop where three dangling balls painted gold announced the business. "It is in this pawn shop."

He flung open the door, and we all crowded into a small space on the other side of it. Some kind of oil lamp cast flickering light in the dark room. A gray-haired man faced us at a counter, wearing an off-white shirt and brown leather vest. Spectacles perched on top of his head.

"Bon soir," Paracelsus said, and followed that greeting with good wishes for the day. I could understand now!

The guy lifted an eyebrow, spoke, and gestured to the chaos behind him: shelves, racks, and trunks, all filled to the brim with stuff. "I have everything you need," he said.

Paracelsus measured a length with his hands, the size of the key. His brows furrowed. "Have you seen a key?"

The man frowned.

"Clearly, we need to show him my key," said Ava.

"Yes, yes, that vould be best," said Paracelsus.

She produced it, and the man's eyes lit up. He pulled the missing key from a drawer behind him, and with it, the missing phone. But he didn't hand them over. "Non, non, non," he said. He rubbed his fingertips together. "Money." He wanted money for them. He'd paid for them. He needed to be paid back.

I didn't have any money, especially not money appropriate for Lyon, France, in 1680.

Paracelsus reached beneath his cloak and pulled out a small brown coin purse. He shook some brass coins into the shopkeeper's hand.

The shopkeeper frowned and shook his head. It wasn't enough.

Paracelsus pulled a small silver coin out of his pocket and laid it in the shopkeeper's open hand beside the brass.

Again the shopkeeper shook his head.

"That is all I have," said Paracelsus with a shrug.

No dice, said the shopkeeper's shake of the head.

How were we ever going to get Nicky back alive, and get out of Lyon?

Ava hesitated and then pulled off her Hello Mellow bracelet. She offered it to the shopkeeper. Gold-colored beads framed a smiling sunny face, embedded on a disk made of enamel. It was a pretty bracelet. She wore it all the time.

In fact, it was her favorite thing. Her face wore a pinched look. Giving it up was surely hard for her.

The shopkeeper weighed it in his hand. "Yes, it will do," he said. He gravely handed over the key and the phone.

Relief poured through my body. Ava and I exchanged a high five, but she wasn't smiling.

A picture flashed through my mind of future archaeologists sifting through old, old trash looking for clues about how people lived in 1680 Lyon, and finding the Hello Mellow bracelet, an artifact of the 2020s. I snickered to myself. Nobody would be able to explain it.

Now what? Martin was no doubt heading back to St. Louis, where he'd demanded we mail him the key. We needed to go there too.

CHAPTER 14
LYON, 1680

WILL STOOD IN the shop's clock room and adjusted a knob on the metal-and-leather mechanism. The mechanism looked like it might operate a very old elevator, with gears and a row of ten or so levers with knobs on the ends. It shouldered into the wall in a back corner of the cluttered room. The thing smelled faintly of well-oiled leather and grease.

"Ach, now that ve have the key, it is time to go to our stop in St. Louis," said Paracelsus, taking hold of one of the levers. "I believe Martin Ortolan vill be going there as vell."

"I want my dog back. I'll mail him his key. You know, just pay the ransom," I said.

"You can't give him the key," Ava told me in that maddening tone that claimed to be right about everything. "Everybody knows you can't pay a ransom to kidnappers. That just encourages them to kidnap more."

"I don't care," I said. "I miss my dog. I want to see him again. And Paracelsus said he doesn't care either."

Ava sniffed.

Paracelsus stepped back and watched as Will moved some levers, and the scene outside the front window changed as the floor jolted just a bit. We looked out on a wide empty street lined with run-down brick warehouses. A parked Prius looked like it rolled right out of the 2020s.

"Here we are," Will said. "St. Louis, earlier in the same day that you left home."

A letter popped through the mail slot with a brief metallic screech, although there wasn't anyone outside to push it through.

Paracelsus scooped it up. "It is for me," he said. After he glanced through it, he looked up. "You are able to handle it from here, Will. The situation in Cush is falling apart again, and so I must go."

Ava and I gaped at him as he bowed to each of us, gestured, and vanished. I wished he didn't keep doing that. And was Will really all that capable? I had my doubts.

The three of us emerged from the shop. It was a St. Louis summer's day, all right, glaringly hot, in contrast to the cool weather in Lyon. I looked back at the clock shop, oddly stuck in the first floor of a brick warehouse that had seen better days. Its mail slot was clearly visible.

My surroundings looked unfamiliar. Was this really somewhere in St. Louis?

Ava scuffed her foot against the brick curb. "I've never been here before," she said.

"I've been here. It's, um, near my house," said Will. "We're just north of downtown. Not many people live right around here anymore. They all moved out to the suburbs."

"Our house is in Webster Groves," I said. A suburb, for sure.

"I guess that's six or seven miles from here," said Will. "It's a long walk. But before we do that, we could look for Martin nearby here, in the caves under downtown."

"Wait," I said. "First we need to go to Webster Groves. Remember the problem with the water overflowing? And we need to get there three years ago."

“Oh, oh right.” Will nodded vigorously. “Let’s go back inside, then.”

We faced the mechanism in the office corner as Will moved three of the ten levers, one of them just a hair. He looked a tad uneasy as he turned to face us with a lopsided grin. “Okay, here goes,” he said.

Did he know what he was doing?

He pushed a button.

Chapter 15
Saint Louis, 2020s

OUR PROGRESS, IF that's what it was, wasn't as smooth this time. The floor jolted a bit as the scene past the front window blurred. Will folded his arms in front of his Cardinals tee shirt, scrunched his eyes shut, and then opened them hopefully.

Where was Paracelsus when we needed him?

This time I did recognize the suburban street scene outside the window. It was Webster Groves, all right. I raced to the door and yanked it open, Ava right behind me. We stepped out on the warm afternoon sidewalk next to a fairly busy road and looked all around. The clock shop now rested in a storefront office.

Just down the street stood the most familiar of buildings, the town supermarket. Cars swished past, cars that also looked to be from the 2020s. Yup, we were home.

Ava and I took turns giving Will a high-five. At several inches taller than me, he ducked his head and looked bashful.

“So, ah, what is the date?” asked Ava.

Will shrugged.

“We could go over to the supermarket and find a newspaper,” I said.

“Bad idea,” said Will. “Remember, the real you is here somewhere and is three years younger. Someone might recognize you.”

"My phone." I pulled it out of my pocket and held down the "on" button. Surely there would be bars now. But no, it was as dead as a pencil.

"My phone, then," said Ava. She pulled hers out of her pocket. Soon it was on, and the icons flicked to life, along with the time and date: 6 p.m. June 6.

So, was that the date we needed to sneak into the house and turn the water off?

Ava and I stared at each other. Will broke our puzzlement. "So is this a good day or not? A good time?"

"I don't know," I croaked. "Maybe we'd better go see."

It was a short walk to our old house. I tried to concentrate. What had I been doing on a summer's day, June 6, in 2019? We had no memory from then of seeing our later selves—giving us the task now of sneaking around.

I risked having my memory tampered with. No, I didn't want that! I shivered.

We three stood on the street and stared at the little house and its white siding, green shutters, narrow driveway, and small yard. Mom's car sat in the driveway. That probably meant Mom was getting ready to leave for work, and Dad hadn't come back from his Uber job yet.

Our younger selves must be inside. Doing what? That was the question.

Eating something? Washing dishes? Sprawled in the living room? Raiding the cookie jar in the kitchen?

Not waiting in line for the bathroom. We didn't have to do that then.

The back patio door was the place to start. Ava and I started for the back yard.

"Uh," said Will. "I don't want to run into your watch dog. I'll just wait out here."

We nodded and kept going as he turned back.

The screen door to the patio was all that separated us from inside. We both peered in. The smell of popcorn wafted out. Microwave popcorn. That's what the eight-year-olds were getting ready to munch on. My stomach rumbled. This time travel thing was exhausting. No time to eat, no time to sleep.

Nicky, the Nicky of three years ago, approached the door from inside, tail wagging.

"It's a good thing Will isn't here," I whispered.

"Yes," Ava said.

"Ava!" a voice in the living room called out. Now, that was weird. That had to be eight-year-old me talking. I sounded squeaky or something. Did I always sound that way?

"What?" came a voice from the far end of the hall.

"Come look at this," eight-year-old me said.

"Just a minute," called eight-year-old Ava.

Well, I clearly wasn't washing dishes, so I wasn't leaving the water running. It wasn't the right moment. But my former life fascinated me.

Beside me, Ava slid the screen door open, grabbed a box of energy bars from the counter, and retreated to the patio. She must be hungry too.

I couldn't resist sticking my hand through the open screen door and giving Nicky a pat. He nudged my hand. That opened a floodgate of feelings inside me. I wanted my dog so much, missed my dog so much.

Did I care if I got caught?

I knelt down, opened the door wider, and gave him a tremendous hug. Ava slipped down beside me and hugged him, too. We were together, in this little spot outside of time. All my jangled nerves soothed and quieted.

Then Will whispered to us from behind, "Okay, time to go." We had to get out before our younger selves showed up in the kitchen.

CHAPTER 16

SAINT LOUIS, 2020S

THE THREE OF us slouched back toward the clock shop, the skip in our steps totally missing. "How'd you pick June 6, anyway?" I asked Will. "When you move those levers, do you really know when you're going to end up?"

He shook his head. "I did my best. It's very difficult to be exact. I suppose Paracelsus would have done a better job. But then, we don't actually know what the right day is. We're guessing."

My hand in my pocket touched one of the mouse-sized guitar picks. I pulled it out as we walked, now passing the crowded supermarket parking lot. "I forgot about these trackers," I said. "I wonder if they can help us."

"Maybe," said Will.

"I don't see how," said Ava.

Soon we sat in the office and wolfed down the energy bars, all eight of them, in five minutes.

I heard the front door open. "I wonder what's in this store?" asked a woman's voice. Then, "Oh, my, too cluttered. Too dusty. Let's go." The door closed.

It was a good thing there wasn't much foot traffic on this section of the street. This being a suburb, people didn't walk places much. Funny, it was a shop that didn't want customers.

"So, Will, where do you usually eat? Or sleep?" I asked. "When you're on assignment, you know? You must get hungry and tired."

"I go back home, usually," said Will. "That's with my dad, in a Native American village with his new wife. But it's pretty weird. The food is strange, and we sleep on mats. I don't feel at home yet."

"So that's why you hang out with Paracelsus," I said.

"I suppose so. Plus, it's fun. And, um, I like rescuing people." He grinned.

Ava muttered to herself. "We have to get back to the house. At the right time. Wish I knew when that was." She shot a glance at me.

"Uh, sorry," I said. "Sorry I don't remember the date." I shuffled my feet. "I know, I know, I can't do anything right." I pillowed my chin on my hand and let out a big breath.

Ava reached over and touched my shoulder. "It's okay," she murmured. "It's okay."

Will pulled some graham crackers out of a drawer. We ate them and took sips from some bottled water he found in a corner.

I stood up. It would feel good to get this whole thing over with. Ever since I'd hugged Nicky, my arms felt empty.

I pulled Martin's key out of my pocket and fingered it. "We'll have to use these, trust the Guiding Hand to get us back to the right instant," I said. "The clock shop can't do it for us."

"Let's use our keys, then," said Ava. "To try to get into the house at the right time."

It felt a little weird to trust the Guiding Hand, who I couldn't see or touch. But he had brought me to the right times and places with the key, so far.

I nodded. "Don't come, Will. Nicky would bark at you."

"I'll wait here," he said.

Ava and I held up our keys and turned them to the left.

* * *

Daylight was fading. We stood at the screen door again, open to the evening air. The television in the living room blared a ball game. That meant Dad was there, hanging out. Eight-year-old me? Eight-year-old Ava? Mom? Not sure. The kitchen was empty. But any of them could show up at any moment.

Was that how it was when I left the water running? Maybe it was. There were others in the house, and no one noticed until it was too late. This could be the right evening.

But we might run into our younger selves. I shivered. Bad things could happen, to me or to Ava.

"Always look out for the other guy," Dad always said. It was time I started doing that. I would take

the risk, not Ava. After all, she'd already given up her bracelet for this adventure.

She reached for the screen handle, but I gently pushed her hand aside and slipped through the door myself. Nicky came up to me and sniffed, then wagged. I patted him. I patted him again. He felt so soft. But I couldn't linger.

Eight-year-old Ava padded into the kitchen, headed for the refrigerator. Her bare feet made almost no sound against the linoleum.

I froze like a cornered rabbit, my heart thumping. Eleven-year-old Ava stepped to the side of the patio door, out of sight.

Eight-year-old Ava pulled some milk out of the refrigerator. She poured herself a glass.

If I didn't move, maybe she wouldn't see me.

She glanced my way. "Jake," she said. "Come on. I can see you. I bet you're after the cookies."

I glanced at the top of the refrigerator. Yup, there was Mom's cookie jar. And now that I was eleven, I could reach it easily.

I gulped and shook my head. "No. Just, ah, petting Nicky." I hoped my voice sounded normal, and I stooped to stroke Nicky's soft ears. It was a good thing I was in a poorly lit part of the room.

"Right," she said, clearly not believing me. "I can tell when you're lying."

Maybe she was the one who wanted cookies. "Here, let me get you one." I reached up, pulled the jar toward me, and deposited it on the counter next to the refrigerator.

"Thanks," she said. "Hey, how did you do that? Did you get taller?"

"Nope," I said. "Not really. Just stood on tiptoe."

She selected a cookie and then left the room, milk in one hand and cookie in the other.

I paused to let my heartbeat settle and glanced at the screen door. Eleven-year-old Ava edged into view and gave me thumbs up.

What if she'd been the one to meet eight-year-old Ava? I didn't want to think about it. It was a good thing I'd come in instead of her.

I retreated to the patio, and we continued to watch.

The dishes sat in the sink. So, who was going to wash them? Ava and I watched my younger self, clad in jeans and tee shirt, wander into the kitchen. Eight-year-old me turned the water on, squirted a stream of dish soap into the sink, and rolled up his sleeves.

The doorbell rang.

My younger self ran to answer it.

Bingo.

I slipped in and turned the water off, then scampered for the screen door, tailed by Nicky. On impulse I stooped and stuck one of the trackers from my pocket on Nicky's collar, before I gave him one last pat and wrenched myself away.

Ava and I slipped outside, held up our keys, and with a flick to the left found ourselves back in the clock shop showroom facing an anxious Will.

CHAPTER 17

SAINT LOUIS, 2020S

IT HARDLY TOOK me a moment to realize things would be different for me now. In the crammed clock shop, I was bouncing up and down, not even worried about bumping into clocks. "We turned the water off!"

Ava and Will reached out, as if to stop my jumping.

Crash! A cuckoo clock fell to the floor. It must have been well-made, because it bounced. The other clocks ticked and whirred, as usual.

Clearly I needed to cut out the jumping. I waved my arms instead.

"And," I said, "I thought of a way to practice with the tracker. I put one on Nicky's collar. It stuck, just like with a key."

"Now, that's an amazing idea." Will pumped his fist. "We should be able to use sixth sense to track Nicky now."

"I already have been," said Ava smugly. "Remember, I just knew he was alive in Lyon?"

I shook my head. "He's had that tracker on for three years." Then I started laughing. They laughed too. It felt so good. I'd done something right.

After I picked up the cuckoo clock, Will stood at the controls. "We'll park the clock shop in its usual place in Vienna and just use the keys now," he said. "We'll trust the Guiding Hand, all the way."

The Guiding Hand. Who or what was he? I wondered. On our money it said, "In God We Trust." Is that what we were doing? A shiver ran up my spine.

We glanced out the window at 1532 Vienna and then moved into the shop's office.

"Let's go!" said Will.

"Yes!" I cried out.

We all held up our keys and turned them to the left. I held my breath.

It was a summer's afternoon. A warm breeze lifted the hair out of my eyes, and the smell of hot asphalt tinged the air. The Gateway Arch loomed to our right, a soaring presence the height of a skyscraper. We had arrived in downtown St. Louis. The cars looked familiar, too. We were home.

Ava narrowed her eyes and swiveled away from the Arch and the river behind it. "Nicky is this way." She set off. Will and I followed.

"Nicky's got to be in the caves, with Martin," I said.

Ava walked fast, and Will and I trotted to catch up.

"Elementary, my dear Jake," she said. "He's this way."

"How do you get to those caves?" I asked Will. "Everybody knows they're are under downtown, but no one knows how to get to them. You live near here. Do you know?"

"From the basements of old houses, I heard." Will shrugged. "I also heard there's a cave under Union Station."

"Let's go to Union Station," I called to Ava. "Maybe we can find a way down to the caves there."

We strode along Market Street for a while. Traffic swept past us, and pedestrians dotted the sidewalks. In the distance, the clock tower on the former train station stood tall against the afternoon sun. I couldn't read the clock, but it must be close to quitting time.

A tall, colorful Ferris wheel stood behind the train station's huge train shed.

"We've got to find a way to the caves underneath there," I said. "Ava, can your sixth sense lead us to a stairwell or something?"

Ava shook her head and grabbed my arm as I passed her. "Not that way. We need to go this way." She'd stopped at an intersection and pushed the button to get a walk light to cross Market Street.

"But, the cave!" I said. "It's over there!"

"Um, aren't we going to the cave?" asked Will.

"No. Nicky is over here somewhere." She crossed the street, striding with purpose.

Will and I shrugged and followed.

We walked away from Union Station for blocks along a wide street lined with buildings. Some people walked there too, some in suits, others with a box for begging. They didn't approach us kids, though. Probably thought we had no money. And of course that was true.

A pigeon soared over my head, coasted to a perch on a light pole, and cooed softly. Pigeons, pigeons, pigeons. Pigeons in Vienna, pigeons in France, pigeons in St. Louis. I was starting to feel like a world traveler.

We kept following Ava until we reached an open grassy field full of colorful nylon tents and the occasional pile of trash. It was a homeless camp. I could see only a few people sitting near their tents in lawn chairs or standing in front of a campfire. Maybe the rest were out and about somewhere.

We stood on the outskirts of the encampment. A cooling breeze swept the day's heat away and lifted the kerchief of a woman wearing jeans as she bent to pet a large dog. Shoulder-length gray hair peeked out from the kerchief.

"Oh, hullo," she said to us.

"Hi." Ava stepped forward. "My name is Ava, and I'm looking for my dog. He's little, a mini Australian shepherd."

"Well, dearie," said the woman, sweeping her gaze over the three of us. "Missing your dog, now, I hate to hear that."

"I think he's nearby," said Ava. "I have a sixth sense."

"Feel free to look around, then," said the woman. "Just be a good neighbor. That's the rule for anybody entering this camp." She seemed to have an air of authority.

"Yes ma'am," we all murmured.

We set out to walk around the edge of the camp, dodging stashes of belongings, tents, and an occasional person. Butterflies rioted in my stomach. "I still think we should look for the cave," I grumbled.

"Oh, be quiet," said Ava. "We're getting warm. I just know it."

I consulted my sixth sense. It appeared to be inactive.

"Why would Nicky be in a homeless camp?" I wondered aloud.

Will chuckled. "Maybe Martin doesn't like keeping him and brought him to some dog sitters here. If Martin is in the caves under downtown, he's not very far away."

Ava began making her way toward the center of the encampment. We followed.

"Nicky!" I called.

"Nicky!" she called.

A bark sounded from one of the tents. A Nicky sort of bark. Some whines. The sound of scratching against nylon.

An older man emerged, and with him came Nicky who barreled out of the tent and into my arms.

I sank to my knees and hugged him.

I had my dog back, and we weren't outside of time. We were right in the 2020s where we lived. My heart felt full. I threw my head back and laughed as Nicky licked my neck and ears.

"Looks like that's your dog," said the man, adjusting the bandana holding his lank hair in place.

"We've been looking all over for him," said Ava. It was her turn to hug Nicky, who covered her face with kisses. "You wouldn't believe it."

"He was stolen." I clenched my hands and released them.

"Figures," said the man. "Thought that kid looked odd. Talked mighty odd too."

Ava put Nicky down. The dog proceeded to run in joyful circles, barking.

Martin stepped forward from a dark space between two tents. He'd ditched the monk's robe and again wore his black jeans, black tee shirt, and silver belt buckle.

He put something into his pocket. He folded his arms in front of him and faced me a few feet away, a head taller and very unhappy.

Oh, no. Was he going to steal Nicky again? Nicky stopped his running and hid behind Ava, peeking out at Martin. She turned and picked him up, thrusting her chin out. Will stood beside her. But I, out in front, stood alone.

"Give me my key," Martin said to me. He held out a hand.

Bandana man looked back and forth between us.

I had lied and messed things up for him. Now, we had the dog. I had to give back the key. It was simple.

I slowly pulled the ornate key out of my pocket and laid it in his hand. The impossible word somehow fell from my lips, like a young bird leaving its nest, beating its wings, rising.

"Sorry," I said.

I truly was.

Martin held the key in his open hand for a minute, looking at me sideways. Then he held it up, walked toward the dark space between tents, and vanished.

That left me facing bandana-man, who had removed his bandana to scratch his head. "That fellow give me the willies," he said. "I coulda swore he just vanished."

"Looked like it," I said cheerfully. "But really, he couldn't have, could he?"

The man looked around behind the tent. "Musta got away, then."

"You were dog-sitting?" asked Will.

"Yup." He shrugged.

I wished I had something to give him for his trouble. Martin certainly wasn't going to pay him for dog sitting now.

Will reached into his pocket and pulled out some cards, lint, and assorted coins. He sifted the cards and pulled one out.

"Aha!" he said. "It's a gift certificate. I knew I still had it. For a free meal at Crown Candy." He pointed northward. "You know it. Um, an eating place not far away, on St. Louis Avenue. Lots of candy and ice cream. And BLTs."

The man's face brightened. "Much obliged."

"Thank you thank you!" I called to him over my shoulder as we set out toward the Arch. Nicky, minus his leash, followed me closely.

We got to a quiet corner. "We can't all go yet because you don't have a key. So wait just a minute," said Will. He held up his key, vanished, and in two seconds returned.

He handed me another key. I held my breath as I picked up Nicky and we all lifted our keys.

Chapter 18
Saint Louis, 2020s

THE EVENING LIGHT in the homeless encampment had given way to velvety night. We stood on the curb in front of our new house, the one with one bathroom. Dad's white car sat in the driveway, visible in the street light. Our brave effort to alter history hadn't changed the fact that we'd moved.

Disappointment curled in my gut. Maybe the move was still all my fault somehow.

The new house, as I well knew, looked a lot like the old one except for black shutters, not green. And it was smaller.

It seemed that we had returned soon after we left, like Will said.

"I'm not going in," said Will. "I'll head out now."

"Thanks for everything," Ava said. "Here, we can give you our keys. For the drawer in the office."

"No, keep them," he said. "You never know when I might need some help."

Ava and I glanced at each other and nodded. We could do that.

He shook my hand, then Ava's, bobbing his head like Paracelsus might. A true apprentice. "It's been good to work with you. See you next time."

He lifted his key up, winked, and vanished into the night.

That vanishing thing still gave me the willies.

I felt sad to see him go. Would we really see him again? But at least we still had the keys.

We turned to walk up to the door. Nicky wriggled until I put him down, and then he ran around and around in circles, barking. I burst into a smile.

Dad appeared at the door in a circle of yellow light. "Nicky!" he said. He knelt and hugged the dog. "Where did you find him? I was just wondering where you were."

"Yeah, we just went out for a walk and got Nicky," said Ava with a grin.

Well, that was true.

"Now, that's a relief." Dad tousled Nicky's ears and led us into the house.

The rock in my stomach got heavier. It was time.

“Uh, Dad,” I said. I gulped.

He turned around and fixed me with his green eyes. “Yes, son?”

Words weren’t coming. I gulped again. Then I remembered. I’d done all those things—chased the dog snatcher across Europe and St. Louis, never giving up. And relying always, always on the team of me and Ava. And we’d succeeded.

If I could do that, was apologizing any harder? No.

I launched into it. “It’s about the guy who stole Nicky. He was looking for a key. I said I didn’t have it. But I really did. I’d picked it up. It was silvery and black. I thought it was cool.” I looked down and shuffled my feet. “I, uh, have to apologize for lying to you.”

“A key, huh?” he lifted an eyebrow. “Do you still have it?”

“No, I don’t. I gave it back to him,” I said.

He bent down to pat Nicky. "I see," he said. "So then you got the dog back."

"Yes."

"Well, I forgive you for lying to me," he said. He tousled my hair. "Just don't do it again, okay?"

I wilted into his hug.

It felt so good to be home.

After a big snack and the usual bedtime read-aloud, for some reason I couldn't sleep.

Thoughts whirred through my head. Did the nerve-wracking trip back three years in time to save the kitchen floor actually make any difference at all?

My body told me it was time to visit the bathroom. So I got up.

It turned out there was a line. Dad was already there. He patted me on the shoulder. "Can't sleep, son?"

"Having trouble."

"Well, you can have my spot in line if Ava ever gets out. Guess she can't sleep either."

"Thanks," I mumbled in response.

"Too bad it's all my fault we have one bathroom now," he chuckled.

Bingo.

He wasn't blaming me anymore.

I didn't have to feel guilty about my foolish mistake with the water. I had really managed to make it right.

I also didn't have to feel guilty about my lie about the key, because we'd made that right too.

When I got back to bed, Nicky had come to visit and sprawled across half my space. I curled up next to him and cuddled him like a teddy bear.

THE END

https://amzn.to/3dHPRbh

Dear Reader,

I hope your family might like to review this book on Amazon (at QR code to the right). I can really use your help spreading the word about my books. Thank you, and God bless you!

Phyllis Wheeler

Looking for a prequel? Sign up for my newsletter at PhyllisWheeler.com, or use the QR code just to the right. This is the only way to get The Grandfather Clock free short story, the prequel for Guardians of Time. It's got rave reviews on Goodreads. You'll enjoy it too.

https://www.phylliswheeler.com/join-my-newsletter/

Made in the USA
Monee, IL
25 February 2023